TALL CLIFF

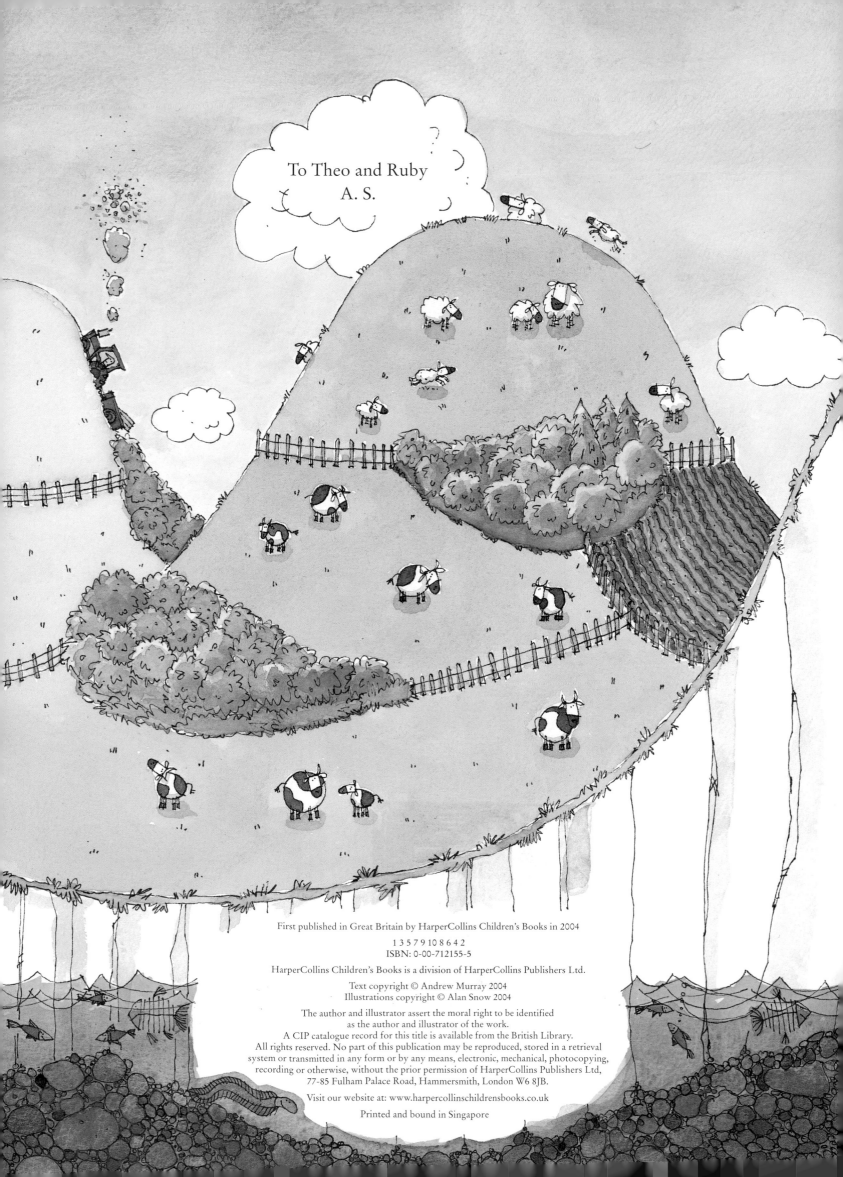

To Theo and Ruby
A. S.

First published in Great Britain by HarperCollins Children's Books in 2004

1 3 5 7 9 10 8 6 4 2
ISBN: 0-00-712155-5

HarperCollins Children's Books is a division of HarperCollins Publishers Ltd.

Text copyright © Andrew Murray 2004
Illustrations copyright © Alan Snow 2004

Visit our website at: www.harpercollinschildrensbooks.co.uk

Printed and bound in Singapore

On a Tall Tall Cliff

by **Andrew Murray**

illustrated by

Alan Snow

Collins

An imprint of HarperCollinsPublishers

On a tall, tall cliff there were two little houses.

The house nearest the edge
was where Puffle lived.
From the edge he could look...

down...

down...

down...

down...

...to the deep, dark
rocks far below.

In the other little house lived Busby.
Busby and Puffle were the very best of friends.

"I'd do anything for you, Busby,"
said Puffle.

"And I'd do anything for you, Puffle,"
said Busby.

One day Busby was busy with lots of papers. "What are all those for?" asked Puffle.

"Nothing," said Busby. "But while you're here, can I ask you a favour? I need to borrow some things from your garden. Your rake…"

"Of course, I'll go and fetch it," said Puffle.
"And your spade, your watering can and all your
flowers and plants," said Busby. "Oh, and your shed,
if you can carry it.

It's a lot to ask.
But it will help!"

"That *is* a lot to ask!" thought Puffle, as he walked home. But he went into his garden and collected…

his rake…

his spade…

his watering can…

all his flowers and plants…

...and his garden shed. He could barely lift it.
Huffing and puffing, Puffle
carried everything
to Busby's
house.

"Thank you, Puffle," said Busby, "but I need to
borrow some things from your house, too.
Your chair
and your table,
your bath,
and your sofa.
Oh, and your bed, if it's not too heavy.

It's a lot to ask.
But it will really help!"

"That certainly *is* a lot to ask!" thought Puffle, as he
walked home. But he went to his house and collected…

…his chair
and his table,
his bath,
his sofa,
and his bed.
It was very heavy!
Sweating and gasping, Puffle carried
everything to Busby's house.

"Thank you so much!" said Busby. "But
I'm afraid I need your roof, too."
"My roof?" cried Puffle.
"Yes, please, and your walls,
and the mice behind them,
your rafters, and the nails in them,
your bricks, and the mortar between them.
And your floorboards,
and the secrets beneath them.
Puffle, I need your whole house.

It's a lot to ask.
But it will really, really help!"

"Busby is making a fool of me," grumbled Puffle,
as he trudged home. But he did everything
that his friend had asked.
He collected…

...his roof, his walls and the mice behind them, his rafters and the nails in them, his bricks and the mortar between them, his floorboards and the secrets beneath them.

Then, huffing and puffing,
sweating and straining,
groaning and grumbling,
he carried his *whole house* to Busby.
"Busby!" gasped Puffle. "This must be enough!
I've brought you my whole house now."

"LISTEN!" said Busby.
There was a rumbling sound.
It was faint at first, but it grew louder…

and louder…

and louder…

"LOOK!" cried Busby.
A cloud of dust rose up as the
edge of the cliff fell…

down…

down…

down…

down…

…to the deep, dark rocks far below.

CRASH!

"Puffle," smiled Busby, "I have been studying our cliff. All these papers and charts told me that the ground where your house stood would crumble and fall.

*My dear friend, you've really, really
helped me to help you!"*

Puffle thought… then he laughed.
"That's true!" he said. "That's very true!"
Puffle rebuilt his little house next to Busby's, and they
lived, the very best of friends, for many long years…

...on that tall, tall cliff,
where you can look from the edge...

down...

down...

down...

down...

...to the deep, dark rocks,
which used to be a cliff,
far below.